This book belongs to:

The Shapeless Shape

by Victor Saad & David Kelley

Illustrated by Edu Vea (NosE)

The Shapeless Shape
20 W. Kinzie
17th Floor
Chicago IL 60654
Or via email at: hello@theshapelessshape.com

Illustration:

Edu Vea (NosE)

Design:

Grip

hellogrip.com

Editor:

Michael Lawrence

Advisor:

Sandra Feder

Shape Maker:

Matthew Hoffman

Photography:

Daniel Kelleghan

First Printing, 2017
ISBN: 978-0-9892230-5-8

To learn more, please visit:

theshapelessshape.com

For those who taught us how to find our way.

In loving memory of Magdi Saad.

Shapes are **everywhere.**

Cities.

Skies.

Nature.

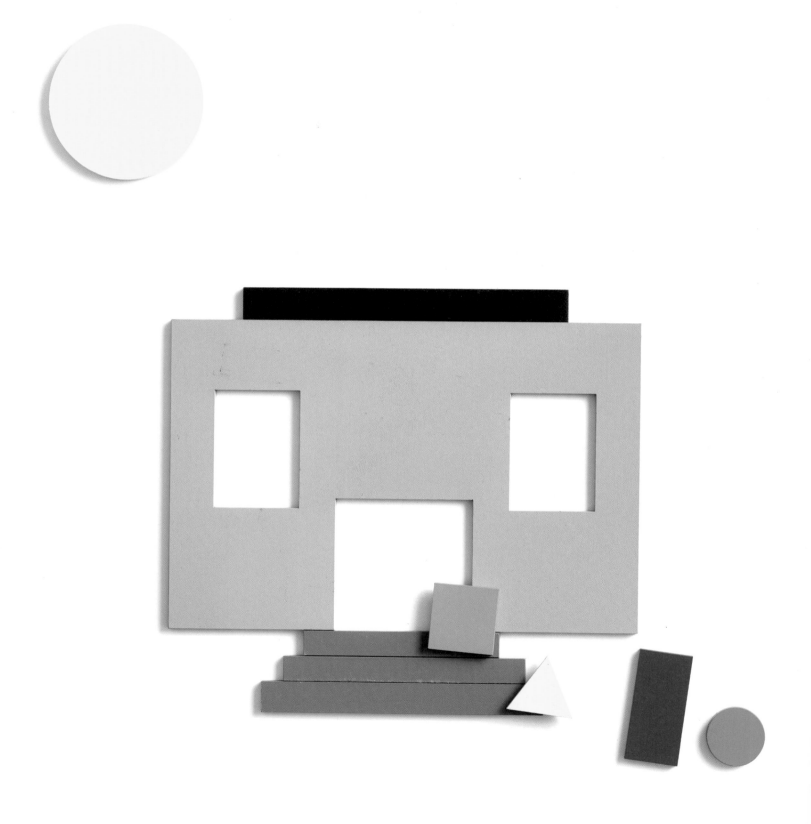

At school, where shapes learn what they can become, there was one shape that looked like no other shape. A shapeless shape.

No one knew what to make with .

 could never make perfect points
like the triangles.

Or make corners just right like the squares.

Or have

5 sides like the pentagons,

6 like the hexagons, or

7 like the heptagons.

The Shapeless Shape went outside
to try rolling with the circles.
And just for a moment, it worked!

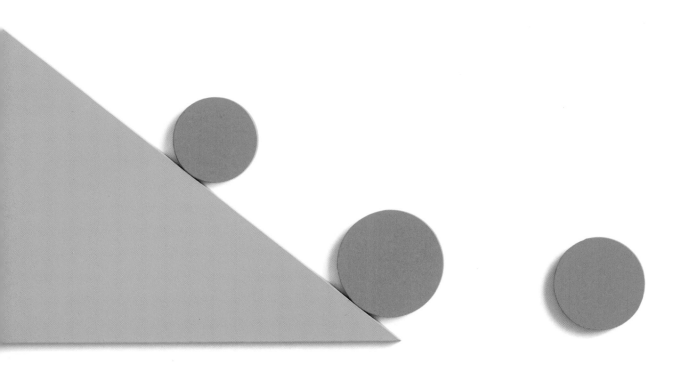 rolled like a perfect circle.

But just when it looked like a fit,
The Shapeless Shape tripped and
crashed into a group of rectangles.

The principal heard the noise. She and
The Shapeless Shape helped the rectangles
stand up straight again.

And when they were finished, 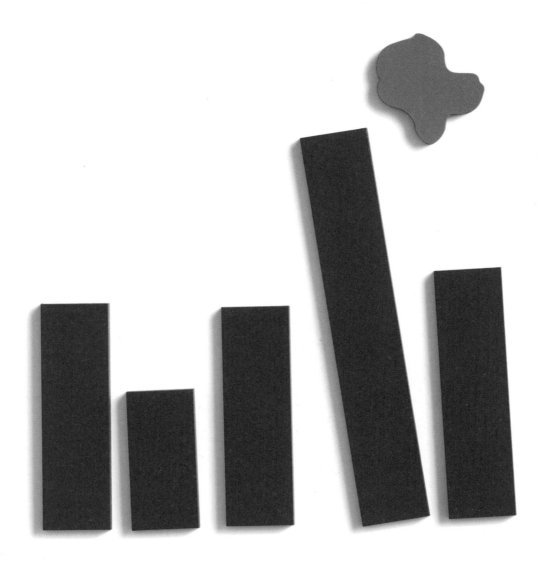 floated
above the shapes to give them shade to enjoy.

The principal saw something special.

"I've known shapes like you," she said kindly.
"Finding where you fit is never easy.
It may take some time, but you'll find a place."

The Shapeless Shape began to search for a place to fit.

 wandered away from school, all through the city, and down a very long trail.

At first, it was exciting.

But soon,  began to feel lost.

The Shapeless Shape tripped and got wet,

and almost got eaten!

But ⬭ was able to float away.

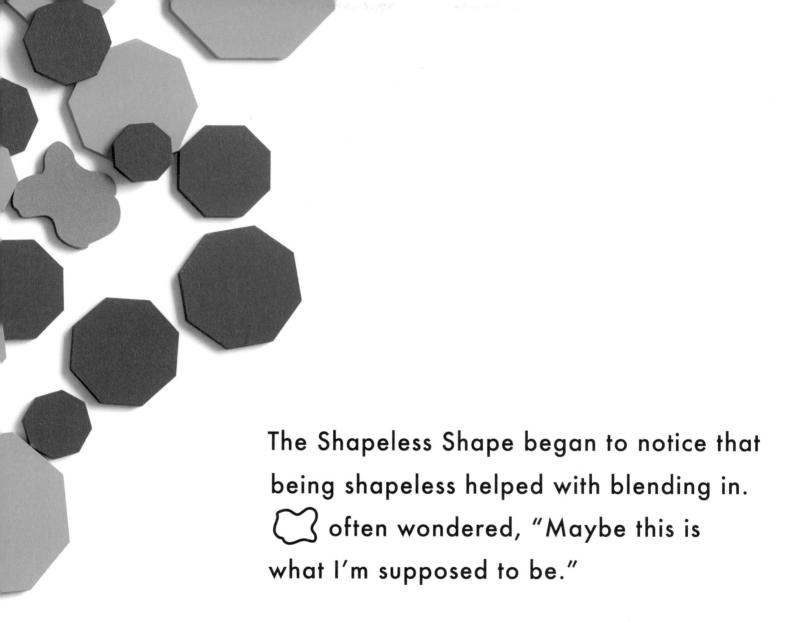

The Shapeless Shape began to notice that being shapeless helped with blending in. often wondered, "Maybe this is what I'm supposed to be."

But nothing felt exactly right.

The Shapeless Shape traveled farther, feeling lonely.

Finally, at the very top of the trail, high enough
to touch the sky, a shape appeared that looked a
little familiar.

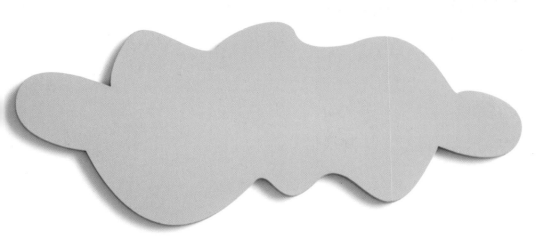

 was excited to see someone else and shouted, "I came a long way, and almost got eaten, but I floated away!"

The new friend replied, "Can you show me how high you can float?"

The Shapeless Shape rose higher than ever before, happily yelling, "Look at me!"

Together, they drifted over the mountain peaks and came to a special place, where shapeless shapes of all forms and sizes were gathered.

"They are just like me!" shouted The Shapeless Shape. "I finally fit!"

shifted, stretched, and soared and realized that shapeless shapes can go anywhere and look like anything.

The Shapeless Shape learned how
to make the rain, and the snow,
and even worked with the sun to decide
how much to shine and how much to
shade each day.

The Shapeless Shape sparked
imagination all over the world.

One day, The Shapeless Shape saw a familiar shape that looked like school, and thought about all the learning that had happened since leaving.

After saying goodbye to all of the new friends,
The Shapeless Shape began the journey back to
the beginning.

The principal saw  coming and went outside to say hello. "It's so nice to see you again. Did you find your place?"

"I did!" said The Shapeless Shape.

"Good," she replied. "Now, you can help me here."

The Shapeless Shape got right to work,
helping circles, squares, triangles,
rectangles, and all shapes learn what
they could become.

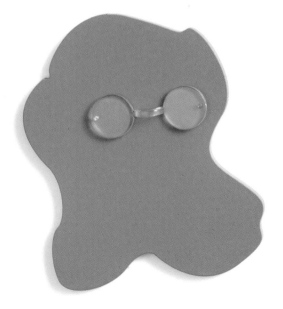

Of course, 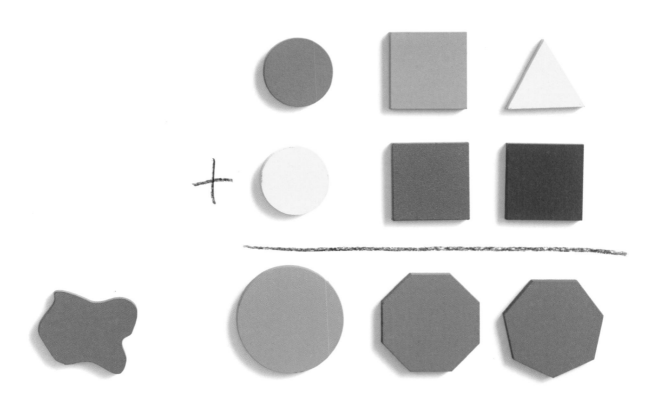 always enjoyed
helping the shapeless shapes the most,
because — with a little help — they
could be anything they wanted to be.

Grip

GRIP is a team of creatives and
strategists solving grand challenges
through thoughtful solutions and
delightful design.

David Kelley

David Kelley is a father, maker,
founder of IDEO, a leading
innovation consultancy, and founder
of Stanford's d.school.

Eduardo Vea Keating

Eduardo Vea Keating (aka: NosE) is
a creative director by day and a
maker by night. His clever style
and minimalistic approach have been
exhibited throughout the US, China,
and Spain, where he's from.

Victor Saad

Victor Saad is an author, educator,
and founder of Experience Institute,
a Chicago-based education company
helping college students & career
professionals learn through
real-world experiences.

Special thanks to:

Manuel Torres for prepping files, Matthew Hoffman for helping to
make the shapes and Daniel Kelleghan for photographing each scene.

Thank you to the Kickstarter Backers
who believed in this project and made
it possible in Fall 2017. You helped
make a small dream a big reality,
and now it's in homes, classrooms,
and offices around the world.